Cowboy Colt

Backyard ⌒ Horses

Dandi Daley Mackall

author of the bestselling Winnie the Horse Gentler series

Tyndale House Publishers, Inc.

Carol Stream, Illinois

Visit Tyndale's website for kids at www.tyndale.com/kids.

You can contact Dandi Daley Mackall through her website at www.dandibooks.com.

TYNDALE and Tyndale's quill logo are registered trademarks of Tyndale House Publishers, Inc.

Cowboy Colt

Designed by Jacqueline L. Nuñez

Edited by Stephanie Rische

Scripture quotations are taken from the *Holy Bible*, New Living Translation, copyright © 1996, 2004, 2007 by Tyndale House Foundation. Used by permission of Tyndale House Publishers, Inc., Carol Stream, Illinois 60188. All rights reserved.

Cowboy Colt is a work of fiction. Where real people, events, establishments, organizations, or locales appear, they are used fictitiously. All other elements of the novel are drawn from the author's imagination.

For manufacturing information regarding this product, please call 1-800-323-9400.

Library of Congress Cataloging-in-Publication Data

Mackall, Dandi Daley.
  Cowboy Colt / Dandi Daley Mackall.
    p. cm. – (Backyard horses)
  ISBN 978-1-4143-3917-7 (sc)
  [1. Best friends–Fiction. 2. Friendship–Fiction. 3. Horses–Fiction. 4. Baseball–Fiction. 5. Deaf–Fiction. 6. Christian life–Fiction.] I. Title.
  PZ7.M1905Co 2011
  [Fic]–dc23   2011015997

Printed in the United States of America

17
7 6 5 4

To Cassandra Eve Hendren, "Cassie"

Backyard horses are the opposite of show horses. They don't have registration papers to prove they're purebred, and they might never win a trophy or ribbon at a horse show. Backyard horses aren't boarded in stables. You can find them in pastures or in backyards. They may be farm horses, fun horses, or simply friends. Backyard horses are often plain and ordinary on the outside . . . but frequently beautiful on the inside.

The Lord said to Samuel, "Don't judge by his appearance or height, for I have rejected him. The Lord doesn't see things the way you see them. People judge by outward appearance, but the Lord looks at the heart."

1 Samuel 16:7

1

Best Friends

"Come on, Dream. You can do it, girl."

I try to sit as still as the sun on my bed. Outside my bedroom window, my new horse, Ellie's Dream, whinnies to me.

My horse. It's still hard to believe I have my own horse. For almost all the nine years of my life, I've prayed for one. And now I have the sweetest pinto in the whole world living right in my own backyard.

Dream is what Larissa calls a "backyard horse."

Larissa Richland is a girl in my fourth-grade class. She makes fun of backyard horses. She keeps *her* horse boarded at a stable in the city. She'd never dream of having a horse without papers to prove what great ancestors it came from. I'm pretty sure she's never ridden anything that wasn't a purebred. And I'm absolutely certain her horse has never set foot in her backyard.

But I can't imagine a better place for my horse than in my own backyard.

Where I live, in Hamilton, Missouri, most people have big yards. But our house sits on the edge of town, the last house in town limits. And our yard is as big as a small pasture.

To make Dream a pen, my dad built fences on three sides of our yard. For the fourth side, he used our house. And my bedroom faces the backyard. That makes Dream's home about as close to mine as you can get.

I scoot to the edge of the bed. I can see Dream just outside my open window. Her buddy, a calico cat, is curled on her back.

"Here, Dream," I call again.

Every morning for the past two weeks, I've tried to get Dream to stick her head through my bedroom window. I used to dream about owning a famous black stallion or a fancy show horse. I imagined him sticking his head in my window to say good night and good morning.

I don't have the stallion or the show horse. But to me, my black-and-white pinto is better than all the black stallions in the world.

I stick my hand out the window. Dream steps closer. I feel her warm breath on my hand. I stroke her white blaze. It's jagged, like a lightning bolt.

Soon her big brown eyes soften. She inches closer. Closer. She stretches out her neck . . .

Knock! Knock! Knock! "Ellie?"

I ignore the knocking at my bedroom door. "It's okay, Dream," I whisper.

Again there's a knock at the door. "Ellie? Ellie!"

Dream backs away from the window and out of my reach. She whinnies. Then, with a bob of her head, she trots off.

"Are you in there?" Dad knocks again.

"Coming, Dad." I drag myself to the door. I was so close! One more step, and Dream would have stuck her head in.

I open the door.

"Oh, good. You're dressed." My dad looks like he hasn't slept all night. "I'll drive you to school. That will give us a couple of extra minutes."

"Dad, I almost got Dream to stick her head in through the window."

"Wouldn't that hurt?" He stands in the door-way and flips through pages of his notepad.

"The *open* window."

"Ah. Much better. And why would you want her head in your window?" he asks.

"Why? Because . . ." I'm not sure. Maybe because it would show she trusts me. "I guess because Dream is my best friend."

"Ah," Dad says again. "But what about Colt?"

What about Colt?

Dad has no idea what a good question this is. Colt Stevens is a boy in my class, and he lives across the street. We both love horses. Colt has been my best friend since kindergarten. Only he hasn't been much of a friend lately. He acts like he's mad at me. And I don't even know why.

"Okay. Dream is my best not-human friend. Besides, I don't think Colt would like sticking his head through my window."

"What? No, I suppose not," Dad answers. He's staring at a page full of exclamation points.

"So what's the trouble, Dad?"

"It's about this rhyme. I need help." He comes in and sits on the foot of my bed. Dad's notepad has scribbles on every page. "I can't seem to get it."

My dad works at Jingle Bells Ad Agency. He has to come up with great ad ideas all the time, or they'll fire him. If the ideas need to rhyme, he usually comes to me for help.

"Okay. Shoot."

"Good. I need a jingle for a used car lot. But not just any jingle, Ellie. My boss wants me to come up with a thirty-second slot for a TV commercial."

"That's great, Dad!"

"Hmmm. It is. That's true. Only I'm fit to be tied. I've been up all night, and I'm out of rhyme. It's a great used car lot too. Owned by the Bear! Can you believe it? I may even get to meet the Bear."

"The Bear?"

"You know. *The Bear*. He's a baseball legend and whatnot."

"And now he sells used cars?" I ask.

"He does. And if I don't come up with a jingle, I may have to ask him for a job. And I'd make a lousy salesman."

"How about 'Go to Bear's Lot—for cars . . . and whatnot'? Just kidding."

"No time to kid, Ellie. This is serious." Dad glances at his watch. "We'd better head for the car. Keep thinking."

"Where's Ethan?" Ethan is my little brother. He's the tallest and nicest kid in second grade. I'm the shortest in fourth.

"Ethan said he'd wait for us in the car."

"Mom?"

"She left for the worm fair."

I don't ask. Mom volunteers for all kinds of things. I guess worms have needs too. I grab my books and follow Dad to the car.

Ethan is in the backseat. I use sign language to

say *Thank you* as I climb into the front. I'm pretty sure it's my turn for the back. But Ethan doesn't keep score.

Ethan puts down the library book he was reading and smiles. It's at least a sixth-grade book. My brother can't talk or hear. But he still makes better grades than I do.

"I'd like the jingle to end with 'the Bear!'" Dad says. Like we all do, Dad signs when he talks so Ethan isn't left out. "Everybody around here knows who the Bear is—everybody except Ellie James, I guess." He laughs a little.

Ethan taps Dad's shoulder. He holds up his hands to let Dad read in the rearview mirror: *Dad, are you making an ad for the Bear? For real?*

"I'm trying to," Dad says.

I know Dad is really worried. A couple of weeks ago, he was up for a promotion. He turned it down. Since then his boss has been crabbier than ever. Mom can't stand for anybody to be mean to Dad. I overheard her tell Dad she'd like to tie Ms. Warden to an anthill and fill her ears with jelly.

"Tell me about the Bear, Dad," I say. It usually helps if I know something about Dad's clients.

"The Bear was number one in baseball years ago. He played for the Kansas City A's before the team moved to Oakland and Kansas City got the Royals," Dad explains. "After that, he did a short stint with the Cards—the St. Louis Cardinals. And he finished out his career back in K. C. as a pitching coach for the Royals. The Bear was number one wherever he went."

He even got number one on his jersey, Ethan signs.

"We have to make people trust him with cars and whatnot, the way they trusted him on the field."

"I'm guessing you don't want me to rhyme *bear* with *mare*?" I ask. This is our little joke. I always try to get horse words into Dad's jingles.

"No horses this time, Ellie."

My brain runs through words that rhyme with *bear*: *prayer, care, share, there, wear, hair, dare, fair, pear, rare, stare, tear, anywhere.*

"Okay." I clear my throat. "For a deal that's fair, when you need some care . . ."

I stop. Out my window I see Colt walking to school. I'm pretty sure he told me his dad was driving him all week.

"Keep going. Keep going," Dad urges.

"Dad, can we stop for Colt?"

"What? Ah. Yes." Dad slams the brakes. "Ellie, finish the rhyme. Please?"

I roll down the window. "Colt, want a ride?"

He checks his watch. Then he climbs into the backseat. He and Ethan exchange *hey*s in sign. Colt learned sign language when I did, just so he could talk with my brother.

"Ellie?" Dad pleads.

"Sorry, Dad. You could end it with something like 'Where can you go? I'll tell you where. To your number one friend. That's the number one Bear.'"

"Yes! Brilliant!" Dad says. The rest of the way to school, he keeps muttering to himself.

I turn to the backseat. Colt is frowning out the window.

"Somebody put grumpy in your cereal this morning?" I ask. This is what my mom says to me when I'm grouchy.

Colt glares my way. Then he turns back to the window.

Ethan raises his eyebrows at me. He taps Colt's arm and signs, *Looking forward to your birthday? One week from tomorrow, right?*

Colt nods his fist to sign, *Yes.* But he doesn't look excited. Ethan and I go crazy before our birthdays.

Colt digs into his backpack and comes out with an envelope. He hands it to me.

I open it. It's an invitation to his birthday party. "Cool! Thanks, Colt."

"My parents made me invite everybody in my class," he says. "I didn't even want a party."

I try not to read too much into that. Colt has invited me to his birthday parties every year since kindergarten. "That's cool," I say because I don't know what else to say.

Colt shrugs. "Whatever."

"Hey," I try, "want to come over and ride Dream after school?"

When he doesn't answer, Ethan does. He signs, *Colt already promised to help me at practice before my game tonight. I want to learn to throw a curve like Colt's.*

Colt still says nothing.

I'm glad he's helping Ethan, though. My

brother joined the county's Youth League baseball team at the end of last season. Ethan doesn't say anything, but I don't think the other kids are very friendly to him. And the coach has called Mom to complain that he doesn't know how to coach a player who can't hear him.

Dad pulls into the school loading zone. Colt is out before Ethan and I get our seat belts off.

"Is Colt all right?" Dad asks.

"Far as I know." I get out and thank Dad for the ride.

The sun is bright, and the sky is clear as I walk into school. But I can't shake the gray cloud that hung over Colt.

Colt Stevens is still my best friend. We've been through a lot together. So I guess it's up to me to cheer him up.

Only I have no idea how.

2

Dreaming

I pull out Colt's invitation. The party is Saturday, a week from tomorrow. It's in the morning, so we'll both have to miss 4-H horsemanship. No wonder Colt didn't want a party.

Tomorrow will be the first time I get to take my own horse to 4-H horsemanship, and I can hardly wait. Every other Saturday before, Colt and I have ridden Mr. Harper's horses. He runs the horsemanship class and owns so many horses that he can let kids without horses practice on some of his.

Colt has been in such a bad mood lately. Maybe a great birthday party is what he needs. And since I'm his best friend, I should come up with the best gift.

Only I need some hints. I race down the hall. Colt is standing outside our classroom. He's staring into the room like there's a lion inside.

"Hey, Colt!" I catch up with him and wave the invitation at him. "So you got any ideas for a great birthday present? I need some hints."

He shrugs.

"Help me out here," I plead. "What do you really want for your—?"

"Colt!" Brooks hollers from the classroom. I can't see him, but I know it's Brooks. His voice sounds like a grown-up's. "You going to stand out in the hall all day?"

Colt lifts his chin in a greeting.

Somebody else calls out, "Colt?"

"Yeah. I'm coming," Colt answers. Then, without a glance at me, without a single word, he goes in.

I stand in the doorway, staring after him.

"What's wrong with you?" Larissa Richland elbows past me. "You look like you lost your best friend."

I frown at her. She grins back.

Rashawn comes running up. Her braids dance around her face. She has the most beautiful hair. When her mother has time, she makes dozens of braids that reach the middle of Rashawn's back. I'm trying to grow out my hair. I want to be able to put it in a ponytail, like our teacher wears.

"Hi, Ellie," Rashawn says. "Did you get Dream to stick her head through your window yet?"

We walk into class together. "Not yet," I admit. "But she's *so* close."

"What are you guys talking about?" Ashley Harper sets her pack down by her desk and comes over to join us. Rashawn and I are wearing jeans and T-shirts. So is Ashley. But her jeans are slim and stretchy. And her T-shirt has sparkles running through it. Her dad is Mr. Harper, our 4-H leader.

"Ellie is training her horse to stick her head right through her bedroom window," Rashawn explains. "Isn't that cool?"

"Wow," Ashley says.

"I haven't pulled it off yet. But Dream will get there. I can reach out the window and pet her now."

"That would be so cool," Ashley says. "Maybe I'd enjoy riding Dad's horses more if I could hang out with them. Like you and Dream do."

I can't believe Ashley's saying this. For years, I've envied her. She can ride any horse in her dad's stable whenever she wants to.

Larissa scoots between Ashley and me. "Are you talking about your little pony, Ellie?"

"Dream isn't a pony, Larissa." I'm trying not to get angry. But she always does this. It's like she can't stand to let Ashley talk to me. "Dream is a horse. And yes, we're talking about–"

"Dream? Is that what you call your pony?" Larissa laughs. "What a cute little name for a pony."

"Dream isn't a pony!" I snap. "She's 14.3. That's 14 hands, 3 inches. I measured her myself. Fifty-nine inches."

"And in case you forgot," Rashawn chimes in, "under 14.2 is a pony. Over 14.2 is a horse."

"Whatever. I'll bet you've never bothered measuring that farm horse of yours," Larissa says to Rashawn. "You'd need a ladder to measure old Rusty."

"Rashawn's horse is named Dusty, Larissa! And you know it," I shout. A couple of heads turn. I lower my voice. "Plus, Dusty is so good-natured. Some people should be more like her."

"Whatever," she says. "So look what I got!" Larissa holds up her invitation as if it's her latest horse trophy. "Colt invited *me* to his birthday party."

I hold up my invitation. "He invited the whole class."

"Even *you*?" She looks at me like I have garbage on my face.

"Of course Colt would invite Ellie," Ashley says to Larissa. "They've been best buddies forever."

Larissa shrugs. "That's not what I hear."

I try not to let on how much it hurts to have Larissa say this about Colt and me. Sure, he's been acting weird lately. But that doesn't mean we're not friends anymore. Even thinking this makes my stomach ache.

"Rashawn!"

"Cassie!"

Both girls squeal and hug as if they haven't

seen each other for weeks. Cassandra Bennet is as popular as Ashley Harper. She could have anybody in fourth grade as her best friend. And she chose Rashawn. Good choice. I'm friends with them too.

Only I'm the *third*. Every time I've been the third friend in a group of three girls, I've always known where I stood. Rashawn and Cassie couldn't be nicer to me. And I'm grateful to have them as friends. But I know they're *best* friends with each other.

Like Ashley and Larissa are best friends.

And Brooks and Dylan.

And Colt and me. Or at least, I thought we were.

"See you later, Ellie!" Ashley calls as Larissa drags her away.

Cassie asks about Dream. She and Rashawn and I talk for a minute. Then the two of them start talking about some TV show they watch.

I wander off to my desk. Around me I hear kids talking and laughing. I realize I haven't said good morning to God yet. So I do that. I think about how Jesus never makes me feel like a third. Mom says my granny's favorite song was "What a Friend We Have in Jesus." Granny's right again.

The bell rings. We settle in while Principal Fishpaw reads announcements and tells us what's for lunch. He tells a joke about two fish. Nobody laughs.

"What is going on?" Miss Hernandez, our teacher, shouts.

I look up to see envelopes flying overhead. One lands on my desk. Somebody grabs it and flings it like a Frisbee across the room. There are at least a dozen envelopes sailing over desks.

Then I realize they're invitations to Colt's party. And he's the one throwing them.

Miss Hernandez grabs an envelope in midair.

She opens it. "What is this?" She reads it silently. "A party invitation?" She frowns at Colt. "Colt, you know our rule about not handing out party invitations in the classroom."

"Yeah," he says.

Miss Hernandez tilts her head to the side. She only does this when she's starting to get angry. She made the no-invitation rule after Larissa brought hers to class. Only, Larissa invited just half of our class. I didn't get an invitation. Neither did a couple of other girls, who cried when they didn't get invited. That's when our teacher said no more invitations.

"Um, Miss Hernandez?" I say. "Colt's inviting everybody. Everyone in class gets an invitation."

Her head straightens up on her shoulders again. "Oh." The mad drains out of her. "Well, I'm glad about that. Still, I'd rather you do this after school. All right?"

Colt shrugs.

School starts for real. We begin with reading, which I love, and move to math, which I don't.

I try to listen to the number questions. But it feels like the numbers float over my head. They don't stay in my brain.

I turn and stare out the window.

I do some of my best daydreaming while looking out this window. Only now that I have my own horse, my daydreams have changed a little.

I wake up, and the first sound I hear is a nicker. It's soft as my pillow. I know it's Ellie's Dream. I go to the window and open it. She sticks her head inside. I kiss her good morning and stroke her blaze. Then I climb out the window and jump on her, bareback. "Let's get Colt," I whisper.

We lope across the road to Colt's. The sun is beginning to rise. And there's Colt, waiting. He's sitting on his quarter horse,

doing rope tricks. He waves his cowboy hat.
We take off at full gallops, my best friend on
his horse and me on mine.

"Ellie?" Miss Hernandez is standing over my desk. "Did you hear the question?"

"I . . . uh . . ." I look behind her, to Colt's desk. He always bails me out at times like this, when I've been daydreaming. I study his fingers, expecting him to start using sign language so I'll know what my teacher is asking me. It's what we do for each other. We sign.

But Colt's not paying attention to me. He's staring out the window himself.

"Ellie?" Miss Hernandez says again.

I clear my throat. Colt doesn't even turn around.

"I think you better stay in for recess. I can explain the assignment for you then."

"Yes, Miss Hernandez." My teacher doesn't act mad like other teachers would. I feel bad that I wasn't paying attention. But if Colt had helped me like usual, everything would have been okay.

Thanks a lot, Colt.

3

Fight

Halfway through recess time, when the rest of the class is outside, Miss Hernandez lets me take a bathroom break. On the way back to my classroom, I pass Ethan's room.

I stop outside his open door. I can't help spying on him. Ethan's teacher, Mrs. Edwards, has the big classroom map pulled down. She's talking about the states next to Missouri. But it doesn't look like the second graders care. Most of the kids are whispering to each other. Some are laughing or trying not to.

Except Ethan. Ethan's chair is the only one in the back row. His tutor, Mr. Hatt, is standing next to him, signing. Ethan glances from Mr. Hatt's fingers to the map and back again. My deaf brother seems to be the only one who is listening.

I walk back to my classroom and whisper to God, "Please give my brother a good friend. Ethan would make anybody a great best friend."

Thinking about best friends makes me think of Colt. And that gets me angry all over again. He had to know our teacher was asking me to name the president from Missouri. I knew the answer too: Harry S. Truman. All Colt had to do was sign the question. After all, didn't I get *him* out of trouble with the flying invitations?

All morning I try to catch Colt's attention. But he won't look at me. At lunch he sits at a table with Dylan and Brooks and Nick. He doesn't even come over and say hi to Rashawn, Cassie, and me.

"Give it up, Ellie," Larissa says. She and Ashley plop down across from me.

"Give what up?" I ask.

"Colt. I see you looking over at his table."

"So?"

"So," she says, plucking a fry from Cassie's plate, "Colt might have been your *buddy* when you were younger. That doesn't mean he still is. People change."

"You don't know what you're talking about, Larissa," I say. But inside, I wonder if she's right.

After school I wait outside for Colt. We almost always walk home together. Even when he's meeting the guys on the ball field after school, Colt and I usually walk that far together. Then I go on home.

I wait until the school yard empties. No Colt. He must have run out of the building before I even made it to the hall.

I need to talk to him. I can't stand feeling like this. Maybe I did something that made him mad at me. I try to think what it could be.

Then I get an idea. What if Colt is jealous about Dream? What if he's upset because I got a horse and he still doesn't have one? For years we've both wanted a horse. We talked about having our own horses and going on long rides together. Now I have one. And he doesn't.

Why didn't I think of this before?

I'm almost to the ball field when I spot Colt. He's sitting alone on the curb across from the field.

"Colt!" I take off running. This is my chance. Colt can act funny when other guys are around. I get that. He doesn't want them to tease him about me being his girlfriend or anything. We're definitely not that. But we *are* friends.

Colt doesn't look at me until I sit down on the curb next to him. When he finally turns my way, his sour frown makes me feel like my nose has turned into a giant snail.

"We need to talk," I begin. "I think I know why you didn't sign when I needed you in class."

"It's not my job to bail you out of everything. Let your mommy or daddy come to your rescue. Or just pay attention yourself."

"Yeah. I know. I shouldn't daydream in class." I don't like his crack about my parents coming to the rescue, but I let it go. I don't want to fight with him.

He shrugs and looks away.

This is harder than I thought. "Something's bothering you, Colt. And I think I know what it is."

He wheels on me. His brown eyes narrow. If he

31

were a horse, his ears would be laid flat back. And I'd be dodging so I wouldn't get bitten. "*Nothing* is bothering me! And if it were, it wouldn't be any of your business!"

"Yes, it would. We're friends. What bothers you bothers me."

He puffs through his nose and turns away.

I try to hold myself together. "I'm not mad about today." At least, I'm trying not to be mad. "I just . . . well, I wondered why you were acting weird. And I think I know. It's about Dream, isn't it?"

"Dream?" He says the word like it tastes bad.

"You feel sad because I have a horse and you don't. But what I want to say is that we can share. You can ride Dream whenever you—"

Colt busts out laughing. But it's not a funny laugh. It's the least funny laugh I've ever heard. "Dream? You think I'm upset because I don't have a nag like Dream?"

That hurts. I try to tell myself he's covering up. "You know you've always wanted a horse."

"Right. I want a quarter horse. I want a horse I can race barrels with. Not a horse that could stand in for one of the barrels."

That does it. I'm on my feet, heart pounding. "Colt Stevens, stop being mean!"

Colt jumps up. He's a head taller than I am. He glares at me. "I'll stop being mean when you stop being short!"

Somebody laughs behind me. I turn to see Dylan, Brooks, and Nick.

Colt's words sting. I know I'm short. I've never really thought of it as a bad thing. People are always telling me I'm "cute." I guess I thought being short was part of being cute, when I thought about it at all. But the way Colt said it makes me wish I could look down on him the way he's looking down on me.

I want to come up with something that will sting back. But my words are clogged up in my throat. And I don't want these boys to see me cry.

I turn and run toward home. I think Colt calls out something after me. But I can't hear him because of the roar in my ears.

Larissa was right. Colt *has* changed. He's not my best friend.

Well, fine. I don't need Colt Stevens. And I don't need a best friend.

4

Advice

By the time I get home, I've given up trying to hold in tears. They flood my eyes, my cheeks, and my neck.

I must have been crying so loud that my mom heard me. There's a tap on my bedroom door, and when I open it, she's standing there.

I throw myself into my mother's arms. I guess it's more like throwing myself into her legs. My mom is taller than most dads. Her jeans are a red blur through my tears. Mom never wears plain old blue jeans. She loves colors too much.

She reaches down and folds me into her arms like she did when I was a little kid and skinned my knee. This time it's my heart that feels skinned.

"Land o' living, gal! You look like death eatin' a soda cracker. What's got your goat, sweetheart?" She strokes my hair without letting me go.

"I . . . I . . ." I'm sobbing too hard to get words out.

"Tell your mama what's troubling you."

I look up at her. Crying makes me madder than ever. "I'm never talking to him again!" I vow.

Mom sits cross-legged on the floor, right there in the hallway. She nearly squashes Squash, our lazy cat, who refuses to move. Mom waves her arms, and the sleeves of her frilly blouse look like flags of all nations, with stripes of every color.

Our dog, Munch, noses around my feet, sniffing my sneakers. Even he can sense something's seriously wrong. He doesn't jump up on me like he usually does. Instead, he plops next to Mom and stares at me like he's waiting for an explanation. He's nearly as big as I am. He eats more than I do. Ethan says if Munch keeps growing, we'll have to move to a bigger house.

"Come sit here and tell me what's got your dander up, Ellie," Mom says. "Who aren't you going to talk to again?"

I sit beside her. "Colt Stevens."

"You and Colt have been best friends a long time," Mom says. With one hand, she's stroking Munch's head. With the other hand, she strokes mine.

"Well, we're not best friends anymore."

"Did you and Colt have a disagreement?"

"You can say that again." I can almost hear him shouting that I should stop being short.

"Friends don't always agree," Mom says.

"It's not that. Colt is acting weird. He won't

37

walk home from school with me. He won't sign. He won't even look at me!" I can't make myself tell Mom everything Colt said.

Mom is quiet for a minute. "Did you ever think Colt might be going through something hard? Maybe you should try to–"

"I've tried! *He* hasn't. And I'm sick and tired of trying. I don't need Colt. I don't need a best friend. I've got Dream."

"Dream," Mom repeats. "Dream is a good friend, all right."

"The best!"

Mom nods like she agrees with me. "Has Dream put her head through your window for you yet?"

"Not yet."

"Doesn't that make you mad as a hornet at her?"

"No." I frown because I know what Mom's getting at. I'm patient with Dream. I should be patient with Colt. "Yeah. Okay. I get it, Mom. But Dream doesn't say mean and rotten things to me and make me feel bad." Tears rise up in my throat. I have to swallow them down.

"I reckon not," she admits, getting to her feet. "Your granny used to say that sometimes you have to be a friend even when you don't have a friend."

"Well, I'm still not speaking to Colt," I say. But it comes out softer this time.

"You know what your granny used to say about giving a body the silent treatment?"

I brace myself for another dose of Granny's wisdom. I barely remember my grandmother. She died when I was little. But she has said more to me than most living grandmothers say to their grand-daughters. "No, what did Granny say about giving somebody the silent treatment?"

"She said it was about as helpful as a back

39

pocket on a T-shirt." Mom walks into the dining room. I follow her.

Dad grins at us from the dining table. This is Dad's office when he works at home. Papers and files are scattered across his side of the table. Dad is always home when I get back from school. He must have heard everything Mom and I said.

"Hey, Ellie!" he calls. "Would you ladies like me to make myself scarce?" Now I know he's been eavesdropping. Dad can't stand arguments. He doesn't even want to hear about them.

I shake my head. "Nope. I was just telling Mom that Colt and I aren't friends anymore."

Dad cracks his knuckles and studies his fingers like he's trying to discover where the sound came from. "I'm not big on advice and whatnot, but I wouldn't give up on Colt if I were you."

Dad isn't kidding about not giving advice. This is a lot for him to say.

"How come, Dad?" I guess I never thought of what I was doing as giving up on Colt. I'd never want anyone, especially Colt, to give up on me.

"People . . . ," Dad begins. "That is to say, humans . . . Things go on in a life and whatnot. And we don't know what."

"What your father is saying," Mom explains, "is that it's not fair to judge a guy until you've walked a mile in his moccasins."

"Huh?" I know I've heard that expression before. But it didn't make sense to me then either.

"As your granny used to say," Mom continues, "friendship can be as slippery as snot on a doorknob. Sometimes you just gotta hang on and hope the thing turns."

I trudge down the hall to my bedroom and wonder what it would be like to come home to normal parents.

5

Pitching

It takes me two minutes to change my shirt and go out to see Dream. My horse is in the far corner of our lot. Pinto Cat, Dream's calico buddy, is lying on her back a few feet away.

I stay quiet and still for a minute. I want to look at my pinto, grazing in my own backyard. She has fattened up in the weeks I've had her. My backyard is big enough to give Dream all the grass and clover she can eat. Her spine still sticks up. But you can hardly see her ribs anymore. Her wavy white mane stirs in the breeze. She switches her long black-and-white tail as if she's directing an orchestra only she can hear.

My horse is the most beautiful horse in the world.

Along with the fence Dad built around our lot, Ethan and I also helped him put up a three-sided lean-to. It's a good shelter for Dream—almost as good as a barn. But she doesn't use it except to eat the Omolene grain I give her twice a day.

"Hey, Dream!" I call.

Instantly she jerks up her head. Her mouth is full, and long blades of grass are sticking out both sides. She looks right at me and whinnies. Even from this far away, I see her sides go in and out with the neigh. She lifts her head and walks toward me.

I head out to her. Then I start running. Dream trots. Then she breaks into a canter. We race toward each other. When she's a few feet away, she slides to a stop.

I throw my arms around her neck and bury my head in her soft, sweet mane. She smells like spring and summer and horse, all rolled into one. I hope God knows how thankful I am for my horse.

There's a big tree stump from when a bad storm knocked over an oak tree last year. I sit on the stump, and Dream hangs her head low enough for me to pet her. "I had a rotten day today, Dream," I tell her. I go over every detail of my fight with Colt, even the worst parts I couldn't make myself tell Mom.

Dream listens. Her fuzzy black ears flick up and back, then side to side. She doesn't give advice. But when I'm done talking, I feel better, like she wasn't the only one listening. Like God was listening too. I guess God and Dream are about the best friends anybody could ever have.

Dream's ears stiffen and freeze forward. She arches her neck and nickers.

I look up and see Ethan walking toward us. He waves.

Before he reaches us, he signs, *I heard about you and Colt. You okay?*

I'm more okay than I was an hour ago, I sign.

He sits next to me on the stump. For a few minutes, he doesn't say anything. Like Dream, Ethan listens in his own way.

After a while, Ethan stands up. *I need to get going. We have practice before the game.*

I'd forgotten about Ethan's baseball game. *You think Coach will let you pitch tonight?*

Ethan's coach is a pretty nice guy. But he's like a lot of people we know. He's sort of afraid of my brother. Coach tends to avoid Ethan. He doesn't give him much of a shot, even though Ethan's a good pitcher. My brother practices all the time.

Mom helps when she can. She's good—she played softball in college. And Colt helps Ethan too. Or at least he used to.

Ethan shrugs. He never complains about not getting put into games. But even Colt says it isn't fair. *Want to come with me?* Ethan signs.

I shake my head. *I'll just go to the game later with Mom and Dad. Okay?*

Dad has to pick somebody up at the airport. He said he'll have to miss most of the game.

Really? I think this will be the first game Dad has missed.

If you come to practice before the game, Ethan says, *maybe you can talk to Colt.*

Colt's coming to practice with you?

Ethan nods. *He's going to help me with my curveball. Colt thought if Coach sees us practicing, maybe he'll let me pitch an inning.*

In all my fuss about Colt being my best friend,

I forgot that Colt is Ethan's friend too. Colt has spent a lot of time with my little brother. Not many fourth-grade guys would help a second grader. Or learn sign language either.

Okay, I sign. *You win.*

An hour later, Ethan and I are at the Hamilton ballpark. Three or four of Ethan's teammates have shown up early to warm up. The game starts in an hour.

Did Colt say what time he'd be here? I ask Ethan. Ethan shakes his head.

Fifteen minutes pass, and still no Colt. Colt knows that Ethan always shows up early. Ethan loves to pitch. He just needs somebody to help him throw something besides a fastball.

Throw to me, Ethan. I put on his glove and toss him the ball.

Ethan throws his fastball and a few slow pitches for the next ten minutes. I'm not a bad player. I can catch. But I'm no pitcher. Colt's great at pitching and hitting.

I keep looking for Colt, hoping he'll turn up. And each time I glance toward the park entrance and he's not there, anger burns another hole inside me.

Finally I see Mom. She comes running up to us. "That pitch looked faster than greased lightning!" Mom glances around. "Colt didn't make it?"

"No," I say, trying not to explode.

"Sorry, honey," she says to me. Then she signs to Ethan, *I'd have hustled over here earlier if I'd known.*

Ethan's coach hollers for his team to gather around. Ethan, of course, doesn't hear him. So I sign the message to my brother, and he runs to join his teammates.

"You look like you've been chewing bumblebees," Mom says.

"I can't believe Colt stood up Ethan! He promised to help him with his curve. Coach will never let Ethan pitch now."

"Don't be too hard on Colt, Ellie," Mom says.

Colt shouldn't be too hard on my brother. That's what I'm thinking. But I keep my thoughts to myself.

Mom and I sit as close to the dugout as they let us. Ethan's Hamilton Hornets are playing the Polo Panthers. It should be an easy win. It would be the ideal game for Coach to give Ethan a chance at pitching.

I watch our team take the field. Ethan and three other Hornets warm the bench. The two on Ethan's left are acting up, elbowing each other and squirting water from their water bottles at each other. Then one of them says something to Jason, the boy on Ethan's right. Whatever he said gets all of them laughing and talking back and forth.

All except Ethan.

To be fair, I don't think Ethan's teammates are trying to be mean to him. They almost never make fun of him. It's just that they act like he isn't there. They talk through him, as if he were invisible. They're careful not to touch Ethan—they don't slap him on the back or give him high fives. Like they think being deaf might spread.

Watching this scene play out—a scene I've watched many times—can make me sad or mad. Tonight, I choose mad. And even if it doesn't make sense, I blame Colt. If he'd shown up for Ethan like he promised, maybe Ethan's teammates would treat him better. The second-grade Hornets look up to Colt, the baseball star. Maybe they'd be nicer to Ethan if they could see that Ethan and Colt were friends.

Some friend.

It's the bottom of the third inning when I think

I hear him. I look over to the basketball courts, and there he is. Colt Stevens. He's laughing with a couple of guys from our class. They're shooting a mini basketball into the hoop.

"What's got you so catawampus, Ellie?" Mom asks.

"That!" I'm off the bleachers and halfway to the basketball court before Mom can stop me.

"Hi, Ellie," Brooks calls.

I don't answer. I'm headed straight for Colt. "Colt Stevens, how dare you do that to my brother!"

"I didn't do anything," he says.

"No kidding!" I shout.

"Oh." He's quiet for a minute. I think he's going to say he's sorry or maybe go tell Ethan how sorry he is. Instead he shrugs.

"You think that's okay? Don't you know how much Ethan wants to pitch? He was counting on you."

Colt doesn't look at me. "With Mr. and Mrs. Perfect Parents, your brother counts on me?" He bounces his little ball and shoots. He misses.

I'm out of words. I could try to live with Colt being mean to me. But not to my brother. Ethan would do anything for Colt. And Colt knows it. "You are a lousy friend. No—worse than that. You're no friend at all."

For a second, I think I see him wince, the way you do when a doctor gives you a shot. It hurts, but the pain is over so fast it's as if there never was a needle.

"You're probably right," Colt says. "I'm no friend at all." He picks up the ball and shoots again.

I must have imagined the flicker of pain on Colt's face.

I turn and walk back to the bleachers. When I let myself look back, Colt is gone.

6

The Bear

Two innings left, and my brother hasn't moved from his spot on the bench. Our team is up by eight runs. Mom and I clap for Ethan's teammates. But I'm pretty sure she's thinking what I'm thinking—why won't Coach put Ethan in to pitch?

"There's your father," Mom says. She stands and whistles through her teeth. "Lenny! Over here!"

Dad waves and walks toward us. A really old guy is following him. It would be just like my dad to pick up some hitchhiker.

"Look!" A man sitting in our row of the bleachers stands and points at Dad. "That's him! Barry, look!"

The man next to him stands too. I recognize him as the father of one of Ethan's teammates. "Oh, man!" He yells to his wife, "Get me something to write on! Hey! Anybody got a baseball?"

Other people are looking at Dad now. A buzz moves through the bleachers. Some of the Panther parents have left their seats to come to our side.

"Hey, Bear!" shouts a kid who might be in high school. "Can I have your autograph?"

Other people yell and wave pieces of paper and magazines and baseballs.

Bear? The *Bear?*

"Mom, that old guy can't be the Bear, can he? He sure doesn't look like a baseball star." He looks like he could be knocked over by the breeze of a fastball. His gray pants are a couple of sizes too big, held up by a skinny leather belt. His arms look like scrawny twigs poking out of a short-sleeved white shirt.

"Use that great imagination of yours, Ellie," Mom whispers. "Picture the Bear about fifty years ago. Your granny had quite a secret crush on him, you know."

Dad makes his way toward the bleachers next to us, and immediately we're surrounded. People shove to get close to the Bear. I could be wrong, but I think he growls. Some guy sticks a baseball in front of the Bear's face. The old man bares his teeth like he might bite it.

The umpire calls a time-out.

"Everybody, please!" Dad shouts. "Go back to your seats. Let the man have some air, okay? He'll be signing autographs at Bear's Used Car Lot next Saturday night. Right after his new TV ad airs. I'm sure the Bear will be happy to sign for you then. Thank you."

With groans and grunts, people go back to their seats. Mom and I scoot over to make room for Dad and the Bear. Dad introduces us.

"The Bear heard I had a son in a Youth League game tonight. He insisted on stopping by with me," Dad explains. "Looks like our side's up by eight runs, eh?"

The Bear has ended up sitting beside me. He stares into my face. His eyebrows are too long, and he's a little scary. "Why aren't you cheering?" he asks me.

"Because they still won't let Ethan play. And he's a decent pitcher."

"Says you," the Bear mutters.

"He is! A friend of mine . . ." I stop because I'm not sure I can call Colt a friend of mine anymore. "Well, a kid in my class who's a really good pitcher says Ethan has a good arm. He just needs to learn how to pitch something besides a fastball. And he needs game time, which this coach never gives him."

"Every kid thinks he can pitch and blames the coach if he can't," the Bear grumbles.

"Ethan doesn't complain. And it is too Coach's fault. He won't play Ethan because he's afraid to coach him. Ethan can't hear or talk. Coach doesn't know what to do with that. So he doesn't do anything. And my brother just sits there on the bench."

The Bear frowns at Dad.

Dad nods.

"You have a talk with that coach?" The Bear says it like he's accusing my dad of something.

"Several," Dad says.

Mom chimes in. "Me too. I'll be hog-tied if I haven't done everything I could to make this coach straighten up and fly right. But Ethan has never gotten to throw a single pitch."

The Bear coughs. He takes a hankie out of his pocket and coughs into it for a full minute. Finally he stands. I don't know why, but he looks taller now. He takes a deep breath and sticks out his chin. I think I can see the baseball legend in him.

"The Bear will return," he announces. Then he walks onto the baseball diamond and stands on the pitcher's mound next to our pitcher. The game comes to a standstill. It's the top of the last inning. The Hornets are in the field with one out on the Panthers. Paul Metzer is still pitching, like always.

The crowd grows quiet as the Bear crosses the diamond again and walks right up to the Hornets' dugout. He shakes Coach's hand, says a few words to him, then walks back over to us and sits down. I don't think anybody's breathing.

At last, Coach shouts, "Time! Ethan James in for Paul Metzer!"

I can't believe it. "How did you . . . ?" I start

to ask. Then I remember. Ethan wouldn't have heard Coach.

"Ethan James!" the umpire shouts.

I look at Ethan. He's still sitting on the bench, swinging his legs.

"Ellie, go!" Mom shouts.

I tear down the bleachers and run all the way to Ethan. Out of breath, I sign, *Ethan, you're up! It's your turn to pitch!*

I have to sign three times before Ethan hops off the bench. He hasn't really warmed up. I wish he'd worked out with Colt. I wish Colt were here now.

Ethan may be the tallest boy on his team, but he looks tiny as he steps onto the mound.

The umpire shouts, "Play ball!" He waves his arm using the universal baseball sign, so I don't have to translate that one.

I stay down by the dugout, where Ethan can

see me sign if he needs to. It's loud here. Kids and parents on both sides are screaming.

"Swing, batter, batter!"

"Wild pitch coming!"

Maybe it's a good thing my brother can't hear.

From the bleachers, one voice stands out. My mother's. I don't turn around, but I know Dad will be trying to calm her down. It won't do any good. She has been waiting all year to see Ethan pitch. She's stored up a year's worth of game chatter. It explodes from her now.

"This kid can't hit, Ethan! He couldn't hit the water if he fell out of the boat!"

Only the kid does hit. He hits Ethan's first pitch all the way out to left field.

Mom hollers, "He's off like a herd of turtles! Throw him out!" But the throw doesn't make it in time, and the kid winds up with a triple.

After that, I manage to blot out everybody

except Ethan. A kid from the Polo Panthers who hasn't gotten a hit yet slugs Ethan's fastball so hard I'm sure it's a home run. But the outfielder catches it at the fence.

Before Ethan gets the last out, he hits one batter with a wild pitch and the Panthers end up scoring four more runs.

The Hornets win. But nobody goes to the mound to congratulate Ethan.

I meet him halfway. *Congratulations,* I sign.

Ethan smiles at me, but he doesn't look happy.

I feel a tap on my shoulder and look up. The Bear is towering over me. "Will you tell your brother he's got talent?"

"That's nice of you, Mr. Bear," I say.

He growls at me. "The Bear doesn't say things to be *nice*! The Bear says the kid has talent!"

As fast as I can, I sign it to Ethan.

Ethan signs, *Thank you,* and I pass it to the Bear.

"Don't thank the Bear!" he roars at Ethan. "You've got an arm on you. The Bear could make it throw strikes."

✫ ✫ ✫

Dad brings the Bear to our house for ice cream after the game. Ethan and the old man act like they've known each other forever. Somehow the Bear is able to "talk" to Ethan without my help half the time.

"What did you say to Ethan's coach that made him put Ethan in?" I ask over our second bowl of chocolate chip.

The Bear almost grins. "I told him I was Ethan's pitching coach."

That night before I go to bed, I try to get Dream to stick her head in my window. She nickers good night to me, but she still doesn't come in. I tell her it's okay. And I tell her good night.

I lie in bed and say my prayers. I imagine God grinning at the way Ethan and the Bear have become friends.

And I wonder if it makes God sad that Colt and I aren't friends anymore. I fall asleep imagining that we are.

7

Whoa!

Saturday morning I'm up before dawn. I open my window and let the cool air finish waking me up. "Dream! Here, girl!"

Dream trots up to the window and stops. We go through our "window dance," with me trying to coax her to stick her head in. She gets close, but she stops short of doing it.

"That's okay, Dream." I reach out and scratch behind her ears. She lowers her head for me. "This is a big day for both of us, girl. Our first horsemanship lesson together."

Over the past three years at 4-H, Mr. Harper has taught me how to ride Western and English. This past year I've ridden English every week, riding one of the three saddle horses he doesn't show.

Colt has never been interested in anything except quarter horses. He likes riding Western. And he'd love to barrel race. That's when a rider competes against other racers and the clock, weaving a pattern around barrels.

For a second I remember the crack Colt made about Dream being one of the barrels. But this time I hear something different behind his words. Colt isn't mean like that. He can act weird, especially when his buddies are around. But he's not mean. I try to picture Colt the last few times I saw him. I think there was something else in his face—sadness.

Colt is sad—really sad—about something. Why couldn't I see that before?

I finger-comb Dream's forelock. "We'll make it up to Colt today. We'll get him out of whatever has him down."

I get dressed and head out to brush Dream. Mom makes me eat breakfast before I go outside, even though I'm not hungry. I scarf down two pieces of toast with peanut butter.

"I should get going," I tell Mom.

"Ellie, it's early yet. The roosters are still dreaming."

"It's going to take me a while to lead Dream out to the fairgrounds." For the three weeks I've owned Dream, I haven't ridden her because I wanted her to fatten up first. I don't want to risk straining her in any way. But I'm hoping Mr. Harper will give me the go-ahead to ride today. "I'm thinking I'll stop by Colt's to see if he wants to walk with me."

"Good idea," Mom says. She's wearing a blue-and-orange shirt with her red jeans. "I'd better get to the fire station." She slips on her red vest that says *Hamilton Fire Department Volunteer.*

Mom leaves, and I bridle Dream. My horse stands perfectly still and even lowers her head for me. I'm so short, I couldn't reach her ears if she didn't help out. I tell myself that even if Mr. Harper doesn't think Dream is ready for me to ride yet, I can still have fun leading my horse.

But I'm itching to ride. I've imagined riding English on Dream in the Hamilton Royal Horse Show. I'd post up and down at the trot and stick to the saddle like Velcro at the canter. And I've imagined racing barrels with Dream, leaning in so far I could touch the ground. I've imagined riding bareback, too. Mr. Harper doesn't let Ashley ride bareback, but Rashawn and Cassie ride bareback all the time.

I snap a lead rope onto Dream's halter. I leave her halter on in case I have to lead her back home instead of riding her. I've practiced leading Dream every day. Standing on her nearside, the left side, I take hold of the rope with my right hand, about eight inches from the snap. My left hand holds the end of the rope. I know better than to loop the rope around my hand. I just fold it a couple of times and grab the center of the fold.

From my spot at Dream's shoulder, I give her the cue to walk on. "Walk." She steps out. I don't have to pull or tug or anything.

When we get to the little gate Dad built into the fence, I say, "Whoa." Dream stops and waits for me to open the gate. I'm fumbling with the lock when Ethan appears and opens it for me.

Thanks, Ethan. Then I see that behind him is the Bear.

"H-hi, Mr.–" I realize I don't know the Bear's real name. "Um. If you're looking for Dad, I think–"

"The Bear has found what he's looking for," he

says. He follows Ethan into the backyard. They're both wearing baseball gloves. Ethan has his baseball.

"Cool." I sign to Ethan, *Have fun*. He grins at me.

Dream follows me through the gate. Pinto Cat hops up onto the fence and balances there, watching us.

Behind me I hear the *smack, smack* of the ball going into mitts.

I wonder if Colt heard about the Bear showing up at Ethan's game. I've determined not to argue with Colt. Or ask him why he let Ethan down. Or why he's been acting weird. I just want things to go back to the way they were.

Dream and I cross the street to Colt's house. Dream follows me into the Stevenses' yard and around to the kitchen door. I hold the lead rope with one hand and knock on the door with the other.

Nobody answers. But I see lights on inside. I knock again. Louder this time.

72

The door opens in the middle of my knock. Colt's mother stands there, one hand on the doorknob. Moira Stevens is thin and pretty, in a fashion model kind of way. She doesn't look like a mother. She's wearing reddish lipstick and glittery eye stuff. Her hair is twisted on top of her head. She is not smiling.

"Hi, Mrs. Stevens," I manage.

She makes an ugly face at my horse and closes the door halfway like I'm planning to bring Dream inside. "Yes?"

"Would you tell Colt I'm out here, please?" I ask.

"Colton isn't here."

"He isn't?"

"No. He's not."

"Ah." I'm smiling so hard I think my lips could drop off. "Okay, then. Thanks."

She nods. I think she smiles, but I'm not sure. Then she shuts the door.

Dream and I set out for the fairgrounds by ourselves. Stupid me. I should have called Colt and told him to wait for me. He's probably already there. Mr. Harper promised Colt he could start riding Galahad, one of their quarter horse geldings. Colt's pretty excited about that. I'll bet he couldn't wait to get started. Maybe riding Galahad will help him not feel so bad about not having a horse of his own.

On the walk to the fairgrounds I have time to think. I remember the day Colt and I became best friends. It was the first day of kindergarten. Already I felt like I didn't belong there. At recess our teacher made Colt and Larissa team captains for some kind of game. I don't even remember what game it was. I do remember Larissa making a big deal out of who she planned to pick—Ashley first. Me, not at all.

After Larissa picked Ashley, it was Colt's turn. I'd already imagined the whole thing—everybody getting picked for a team except me. Then Colt hollered out, "Ellie!"

I never asked him why he picked me first that day. But I never forgot it.

I have to get us back to being best friends.

"One week from today is Colt's birthday," I tell Dream. I tune in to the steady clip-clop of her hooves. The morning is already warming up. When I stroke Dream's neck, the hairs feel warm to the touch.

"I'm Colt's best friend, whether he likes it or not," I continue. "That means I have to come up with the best birthday gift." It makes sense. "Only, what can I get him, Dream?"

Again, the clip-clop of her hooves plays like music in my brain.

"Colt has all the baseball and sports gear he could ever want. I don't even know the names of all his games and electronic devices."

Dream bobs her head up and down without losing stride. Her black-and-white tail flicks a fly off her rump.

"Colt has everything, Dream."

She huffs out a tiny sound. A sneeze or a whicker.

My cloudy brain clears. "Everything except a horse." I stop. Dream stops beside me. I throw my arms around her neck and kiss one of her black spots. "That's it, girl! I have to get Colt a horse for his birthday!"

8

Horsemanship

As soon as I see the fairgrounds, I take off at a jog. Dream trots easily beside me. I don't know what I'm more excited about—the possibility of riding my horse for the first time or the thought of surprising Colt with a horse for his birthday. I just hope I can keep it a secret.

I'm not stupid. I know horses cost money. And I know I don't have much of it. But I do have some. And maybe I could borrow the rest from my parents and pay them back a little at a time.

"Ellie!" Rashawn shouts across the field. She looks tiny sitting on Dusty. We're not sure what breed Dusty is, but she's a dapple-gray plow horse. Or at least her parents were plow horses.

"Rashawn!" I wave at her. Next to Rashawn, Cassandra is on her little black pony, Misty. They're both riding bareback. "Cassie!" I holler.

Dream and I keep jogging until we meet Cassie and Rashawn at the arena. "I can't believe you guys are here already."

"We couldn't wait to see you and Dream," Rashawn says.

That makes me feel pretty good. They're terrific friends, even if I am the third wheel. "I hope Mr. Harper says it's okay to ride Dream." I look at my horse and stroke her jawline with my finger.

"I bet he will," Cassie says. She nudges her pony to come closer. It takes a couple of squeezes with her knees. Misty can be stubborn sometimes.

"She looks great, Ellie. She's really put on a lot of weight. In a good way," she adds quickly.

"Is Mr. Harper here yet?" I can't wait to get the okay to ride.

Rashawn shakes her head. "Just us. Nobody else yet."

"Except Colt, right?" I look around. "Where is he?"

"Colt?" Cassie frowns at Rashawn. "I haven't seen him. Have you?"

"He's not here yet," Rashawn says.

"Are you sure? I stopped by his house. He wasn't home."

"There he is!" Cassie shouts. She urges her pony forward, a step at a time.

I turn, expecting to see Colt. But it's Mr. Harper. He's driving his truck with the four-horse trailer hitched behind it. I sure hope I won't be needing one of his riding horses. I want to ride my Dream.

The second Mr. Harper and Ashley step out of the truck, I'm waiting for them. "So? What do you think, Mr. Harper? Is Dream ready yet?"

He takes one look at her. "Ellie, it's hard to believe this is the scraggly mare that had us running all over town trying to catch her. You've done a good job fattening her up. I'd say you're good to go."

"Yes!" I hug my horse.

He tosses me a safety helmet and asks if I want to borrow a saddle. But I decide to ride bareback, like my buddies.

The other 4-H riders start showing up, about a dozen kids riding in from all directions. Mr. Harper saddles Hancock's Warrior, a bay jumper, for Ashley. Two girls don't have horses of their own. So one takes a gentle saddle horse I've ridden lots of times before, and the other mounts a Tennessee walking horse I've ridden once.

"Where's Colt?" Mr. Harper asks.

"I guess he isn't here yet." I look around the field again. No Colt.

"I hope he shows. I brought Galahad for him." He grins at me. "But I think we have more important things to think about now. Ellie, how would you like a boost up on your new horse?"

The instant I slide onto Dream's back, I feel like I belong here. It's like my legs and her sides were made to fit together like this. The only problem is that her spine is still a little too sharp for comfort. But I know it will soften up as she puts on more weight.

"Um . . . maybe I'll take you up on that offer to borrow a saddle, Mr. Harper."

Cassie and I borrow English saddles, and Rashawn borrows a Western saddle with an extra-long cinch.

I mount without any help. I am so grateful to

be sitting on my own horse. *Thanks, God. Thank You, thank You, thank You.*

"Way to go, Ellie!" somebody shouts. It's Miranda, a sixth grader, who rides an Appaloosa that's solid brown on the front half but spotted on its rump.

Other kids shout out congratulations too.

Then Dream and I ride into the arena for our first horsemanship lesson. The rest of the morning is a joyful blur. Mr. Harper shouts out instructions as we circle the arena.

"Balance, balance, balance!"

"Check your position! Don't let your ankles cave in. Toes pointed in."

"Sit tall in the saddle, people! Look up and past your horse's ears."

"Relax your arms. Elbows close, but not touching."

"Don't forget to breathe! Your horse will pick up your tension."

After a while, though, it all becomes natural. Dream and I simply ride, enjoying each other's friendship.

☆ ☆ ☆

I'm the last one to leave the fairgrounds when the lesson ends. I hang around the Harper trailer while they load their horses.

"I can't believe Colt didn't show," I tell Mr. Harper. "I know how psyched he's been about working with Galahad." Galahad is a young gelding, but he'll make a super cutting horse. Quarter horses usually make the best barrel racers.

"Well, there will be other chances. I'm sorry I had to cancel horsemanship next Saturday, though." Mr. Harper unties the last rope from his trailer. "I can't let Ashley miss that Breckenridge show. Too many points at stake, and that show's in our circuit."

"That's okay, Mr. Harper. It's Colt's birthday party on Saturday anyway."

As Mr. Harper leads the saddle horses into the trailer, I imagine it's a week from today, Colt's birthday.

The whole class has turned out for Colt's birthday party, except Ashley, who has to go to the horse show. It's a perfect day—sunny and warm but not too hot. One by one, Colt unwraps gifts from our classmates. There's only one left, the gift from his best friend. Me.

"Come outside, Colt," I tell him.

He frowns, but he follows me out to his backyard. And there stands Galahad, the beautiful bay quarter horse.

"Mr. Harper, how much would Galahad, or a horse like Galahad, cost?" I ask.

He stops what he's doing and eyes the quarter horse. "I don't think I have a mind to sell Galahad. He's a good one. I think he's going to make a great barrel racer. But I imagine any good cutting horse would go for a few thousand dollars or more."

"A few . . . ?" I can't finish. I knew a registered quarter horse would cost a lot of money. Only I didn't know it would cost *that* much.

How am I going to come up with that kind of money?

9

Gift Horse

I should be totally thankful and happy as I ride home. And I am. I got to ride my own horse at 4-H horsemanship. Dream did everything right too.

Not only that, but Larissa never showed up. One more thing to be thankful for.

Only I can't stop thinking about getting a horse for Colt. I'll never be able to afford a horse, especially a quarter horse like Colt wants.

I ride the first half of the trip home using a saddle from Mr. Harper and lead Dream the last half to cool her off. When we get to my backyard, I brush her dry and thank her for giving me the best ride of my life.

Ethan and the Bear are still throwing pitches. Actually, they look like they're mostly talking. Except Ethan doesn't speak, and the Bear can't sign.

I wave to them, then go inside so I can get to work finding Colt a horse. First, I start searching the Internet, but all the horses are too expensive and too far from Hamilton anyway. Finally I give up on cyberspace and set up an office at the dining table, like Dad does. Armed with old copies of our local newspaper, I track down every lead.

Every horse listed in the paper is too expensive. I call about all the ads that don't give a price, and they're asking for even more than the others.

When Mom gets home from the fire station, I tell her my plan . . . and the problem with my plan.

"I see what you mean," she says. She hangs up

her fire station volunteer gear. "But as your granny used to say, there's more than one way to skin a cat."

It's a nasty saying. But I'm pretty sure it means there may be other ways to get my friend a horse.

"What about getting a horse from one of the animal shelters?" I ask.

"The shelters I know of are sending horses to that wildlife refuge down south, in the Ozarks," Mom says. "I'll make some calls. But don't get your hopes up."

But I have to keep my hopes up. After all, we got Dream from a cat farm. Horse miracles do happen. And if they can happen once, why can't they happen twice?

"Are those two still at it?" Mom asks, staring out the back window.

We watch them huddle, then come away and pitch, then huddle again. "The Bear doesn't know sign language, does he?" I ask.

"I don't think so." Mom gets two bottles of water and tosses them to me.

I take the water outside and offer to sign for Ethan and the Bear.

The Bear takes his water and downs it in one gulp. For the next fifteen minutes he barks orders at me as if I'm the one pitching. I sign to Ethan:

No rainbow tosses. Straight and flat, even in warm-ups.

Most kids finish a pitch with their arm next to their waist. Don't! Bend that knee and keep going.

The Bear drops his hat beside Ethan's left foot and tells him to pick up the hat after every delivery. I watch a few pitches, followed by hat pickups. It works. Ethan's pitches are straighter and faster than ever.

They both do what the Bear calls a flamingo drill. He makes me do it too. We stand with one knee lifted, trying to keep our balance, and stay in that position as long as we can.

In flamingo position, I ask the Bear, "What about a curveball? Our friend Colt was going to help Ethan with his curve."

"No curve!" the Bear shouts. "No slider! No junk!" Even with all the shouting, he hasn't lost his balance. He keeps standing on one leg, the other knee bent. "Throwing junk is how kids hurt their arms!"

Ethan signs, *The Bear is teaching me a changeup pitch instead of a curve. No stress on the arm with a changeup.*

Ethan jogs to a little mound they've built in the backyard. He throws a couple of pitches that I assume are changeups. They look slow.

I would hate for Ethan to ruin his arm when he is only in second grade. Maybe it's a good thing Colt didn't help Ethan with a curveball after all. I was so mad at him when he didn't show up to help my brother before the ball game. I was even a little mad at God for letting Ethan get stood up like that. But maybe God was looking out for Ethan's arm all along.

"Girl!" The Bear's shout brings me back. "Did you hear what I just said?"

"What?" I glance at him, then at Ethan. I have no idea what I'm supposed to be signing. "Sorry."

Ethan takes off his glove and jogs over to me. *What's wrong, Ellie?* he signs.

I shake my head. "It's Colt."

Did you two fight again?

"No. I want to get him a horse for his birthday. But I don't have the money. I guess it's a crazy idea."

"You got yourself a horse," the Bear interrupts. "How'd you swing that?"

I sign the Bear's words to Ethan. He nods. "I prayed for it. But it took years and years. This time I only have a week."

A sound comes from the Bear's mouth. At first I think it's a giant roar. Then I realize . . . it's laughter. He laughs until tears stream down his face. When he's done, he says, "All this fuss is over a horse you don't got?"

"Yeah," I admit.

"You need a horse. I have one I need to get rid of."

"You have a horse?" Somehow I can't picture the Bear on a horse.

"I do. But I don't get down to the ranch much anymore. I've been trying to find the old boy a good home."

Old boy. I picture a horse that looks kind of like the Bear, old and frail. "How old is your horse?"

"About fifteen, I reckon."

Fifteen isn't that old for a horse. Not if the horse has been taken care of.

I sign to Ethan, *Did you pray for a horse for Colt?*

Nope. It's all you, Sis. And you must be getting better at it. It didn't take you seven years this time. He laughs, a sweet noise that sounds like it comes directly from his heart.

I'm afraid to get excited about this. I want to ask the Bear more questions. Has he taken good care of the horse? What kind of horse is it? But Granny used to say you should never look a gift horse in the mouth, meaning don't be ungrateful about something you've been given for free. So I keep my mouth shut.

Ethan must be on my wavelength, though. He signs, *What kind of horse is it?*

The Bear waits until I'm done interpreting Ethan's question. Then he answers, "A cow horse. Ol' Bullet might not be much to look at. But he's got heart. And heart can take you a long way in just about any business."

10

Secrets

The rest of the weekend I can't think of anything but the fact that I'm going to have the best gift for my best friend. A cow horse. I'm guessing it's probably at least part quarter horse. That's what Colt has always wanted.

Dad thinks I should talk to Colt's parents to make sure it's okay. But I know it will be. They have lots of space. And plenty of money for vets and farriers and feed too. Mom ended the discussion by agreeing with me. "I think a horse might be the best thing to happen to Colt in a month of Sundays."

The only problem I can see is how I'm going to keep my gift a secret from Colt until his birthday. I'm afraid if he asks me anything, I'll spill the surprise at school on Monday.

But as it turns out, this isn't a problem. Colt doesn't show up at school on Monday. After school I jot down all the assignments for him. I bring home my books for him to use too. It's what we've done for each other since first grade.

It's not easy lugging everything over to his house. I trudge up to the Stevenses' front door and ring the doorbell. Nobody comes to the door. I didn't expect Colt's dad to be home. I'm not sure where he works. He's gone a lot. But I kind of thought Mrs. Stevens would be home. When I'm home sick from school and Mom can't stay with me, Dad takes off work. And Colt's mom works at the same place as Dad, the Jingle Bells Ad Agency.

I ring the bell again. No answer.

I think about leaving the stuff for Colt on their porch, but it looks like it's starting to rain. I grab my books and dash across the street just as the sky opens up. I'm soaking wet when I crash into our house.

Dad pulls the door open before I can. "You look like you could use something hot to drink," he says.

Dad, Ethan, and I are sipping homemade hot chocolate when Mom rushes in. She's drenched. Whatever dress she's wearing is bleeding colors all over the kitchen floor.

"Whoo-whee!" she exclaims. "It's raining so hard out there I believe the animals are pairing up. And if I didn't know our neighbors so well, I'd think they were getting into the ark business.

Somebody's building something over at the Stevenses' place."

Now that she mentions it, I did see a bunch of lumber piled up in their yard.

I get Mom a beach towel. Dad makes her a cup of hot chocolate. And Ethan gets her slippers.

While Mom sits down to sip her hot chocolate, I go to the front window and look across the street. A wood frame is already put together in the back of Colt's yard. I hope they don't plan on building another house there. It's a big yard, but I wouldn't want Colt's new horse to have to share the lot.

I keep an eye out for Mrs. Stevens to come home. Twice I call Colt, but nobody answers. I don't call anymore because I don't want to wake him. But I wish he had somebody there with him. Maybe he's just a little bit sick.

It's getting dark when Mrs. Stevens's car finally

comes around the corner. I tear across the street, glad it has stopped raining. I call her name, but I don't think she hears me. She pulls into their garage. The automatic garage door starts closing just as I get there. I duck under it, and the door rises automatically.

Mrs. Stevens gets out with her briefcase. She doesn't look surprised to see me in her garage. "Ellie?"

"Is Colt okay?" I ask. I was in such a hurry that I forgot the bag of books for Colt.

"Yes," she answers.

"That's good. Um, I have his assignments. You know, so he won't get behind. Only I left them at my house."

"Thoughtful," she says. "But unnecessary."

"Huh?"

"Colt already has his assignments for the week."

"Is he that sick?" I want to ask if I can see him.

"He's not sick at all," she explains.

"But you said–"

Mrs. Stevens blows out air the way horses do when they're getting riled. "Colt and Sierra are spending the week in St. Louis. With their father." I start to ask why, but she cuts me off. "Thank you for your concern, though." She puts one hand on the garage door opener.

I turn and leave the garage. The door closes behind me.

When I get home, I hear Dad and the Bear discussing the used car commercial. Mostly it's the Bear talking. He stays to eat a late dinner with us.

I fill everybody in on Colt's mysterious St. Louis trip with his dad. "I don't get it. Why would he and his sister miss a whole week of school? Why would their parents let them?"

Mom and Dad exchange looks. Ethan and I

think they have their own sign language. They talk with their eyes.

"What?" I know they know something. "What aren't you telling me? Colt is *my* friend. I have a right to know."

"If he'll be back in a week, I guess you can ask him yourself then," Dad says. "Please pass those yummy mashed potatoes."

I turn my gaze to Mom. She zips her lips closed, then swallows the invisible key. I get it. They're not talking.

11

Bullet

Wednesday after supper Ethan and I sit on our front porch to wait for the Bear. He flew all the way to his ranch in Tulsa, Oklahoma, on Tuesday just to pick up his horse. Now it's taking him all day to drive back with his horse trailer.

After a while, the sun goes down and the moon rises. A low whine of crickets starts up. I describe this to Ethan the best I can. A dog is barking far away somewhere. Munch hears it from inside our house and barks back.

Sometimes I think about this whole world of

sound that Ethan misses out on, and it makes me sad. But I know God makes it up to him in ways the rest of us can't understand.

Are you sure Colt's mother doesn't know you're giving him a horse? Ethan signs.

I'm sure.

But doesn't that look like a barn to you?

Ethan's right. All day long, eight men hammered away at what's starting to look like the frame for a two-story barn. Colt's backyard is almost twice as big as ours. It's already fenced in too. How great would that be if they were putting up a barn!

There he is! Ethan signs.

A rusty, beat-up tan-and-silver horse trailer bounces along our road. It's too dark to see into the cab of the truck pulling it. But it's got to be the Bear behind the wheel.

He pulls into our driveway. Ethan and I run

to meet him. I go straight to the back of the trailer and peer in. It's dark. All I can see is that the horse is about Dream's height.

"Out of the way," the Bear roars.

I step back to give him room to put down the tailgate. "Why did you name him Bullet?" I ask. Ethan asked me that while we were sitting on the step. But I want to know too.

"He used to be fast as a speeding bullet." The Bear walks up the tailgate plank.

"Colt loves to ride fast," I say, getting even more excited.

Inside the trailer, something rattles. The trailer rocks. The Bear says, "Back!" And hooves *clang, clang* on the tailgate as the horse backs down the plank onto the driveway.

I stare at what looks like a gray ball of horse. *Maybe it's because it's so dark,* I tell myself. *Maybe in the light of day . . .*

"I warned you he wasn't much to look at," the Bear says.

I remember what Colt said about my horse looking more like a barrel than a barrel horse. He was wrong. But if any horse ever did look like a barrel, it would be this one. His sides stick out, and his belly looks too close to the ground. He's the fattest horse I've ever seen.

"My foreman's a lazy good-for-nothing," the Bear growls. "He left ol' Bullet here out to pasture night and day through the spring. And that's a rich pasture. I admit it's going on three years since I was at the ranch. Bullet put on a few pounds."

A few hundred pounds, I think. I have the Bear and Bullet follow me into the backyard. When I open the gate, Dream nickers and starts trotting toward me.

Then she stops. I can tell by the way she's

standing that her ears are back. Her nostrils are wide. I hear her foreleg pawing the ground. She does not like this newcomer.

"It's okay, Dream," I call out. "We have a friend for you."

Bullet whinnies. His whole chest jiggles like a barrel full of jelly. I walk over to him and stroke his neck. I should have given him a better greeting right off. "Don't worry, Bullet," I murmur. His neck is firm. Muscled. It surprises me.

Dream whinnies at Bullet. But it doesn't sound like a warm greeting.

Bullet answers with a whimper.

"Okay," I admit, stroking his neck. "Maybe we don't have a friend for you quite yet."

Dream watches as we put Bullet in the lean-to. The Bear ties him in.

"The last thing this horse needs is fresh clover," he says.

I know he's right. But I still think every horse should have food around almost all the time. "We have hay in Dad's shed," I tell the Bear. "It's low calorie, compared to grass and grain."

I sign to Ethan, and he brings Bullet an armful of hay to munch on overnight. He signs to me, *Thanks, Bear, for driving all the way to your ranch. And thanks for giving us your horse.*

Ethan has a point. I thank the Bear for everything.

The Bear walks into the lean-to and checks Bullet's rope. Ethan has already untied the Bear's knot and replaced it with one of his own quick releases. Ethan is great with knots. "Nice," the Bear mutters.

Dream stops pawing the ground. She does a half rear and takes off. Bucking and thrashing, she circles the yard. Then she slides to a halt a good distance from the lean-to and snorts. Again she paws the ground and lets out a whinny that sounds like a threat.

This time Bullet paws the ground and snorts in response.

Even Pinto Cat arches her back and hisses at Bullet from the safety of Dream's side of the yard.

"Hey! You guys are supposed to be friends," I tell them.

The Bear stares from Dream to Bullet and back. "Long way from being friends. I'd say they're arguing."

And I'd say they remind me of Colt and me.

As I fall asleep that night, I try to imagine riding with Colt—me on Dream and Colt on Bullet. But the dream keeps fading. Even I am having trouble imagining that inside that round barrel of horse, a real quarter horse is waiting to come out.

12

Changeups

The next morning I get up early enough to take Dream out for a short ride before school. I've dreamed about doing this. And now my dream has come true.

I just hope Colt feels the same way when I give him his horse on his birthday.

Dream and I head out of town. About a block from home, the gravel road turns to dirt. The sun is shining through the trees. Birds are singing. I hear a mourning dove, a woodpecker, a cardinal, and a lot of other chirping.

As if my horse can read my mind, she breaks into a canter, slow and easy.

I can imagine all kinds of things. But I can't imagine life getting any better than this moment right now. Everything in me feels thankful. And I wonder if it can be worship to be sitting on a pinto, feeling the morning breeze, and hearing the pounding of hooves on a dirt road.

After my ride, I brush Dream. Then I check on Bullet. "How's it going, ol' boy?"

I turn him out to the backyard. He goes straight for the grass. I run my hand down his neck, back, and hip. They feel equal in length. That's something to look for in a horse. It means good balance.

I move back to his head and scratch behind his ears. Dream loves this, but I guess Bullet doesn't. He flicks his ears and pulls his head away. I keep scratching until I find a spot right under his jaw.

When I scratch there, he closes his eyes halfway and relaxes. "You like that, don't you, boy?"

I take my time examining Bullet's head. Small ears. Broad between the eyes. The only slender part on this horse is at the throat, where the halter's throatlatch goes. He has a nice, clean line there. I know that's a good sign—it usually means the horse can bend his head and neck easily. That's important for a barrel horse.

Flecks of white are sprinkled through the gray on his face, like white freckles. But he has a pretty face. A good head.

I back up and get an overall look at Bullet. It's hard to see past the fat and roundness. But his body is square. That's something Mr. Harper says he looks for in a quarter horse. Plus, his legs are straight and not too fine boned. Bullet has good shoulders. Solid withers. And a strong back, even if it is too round and broad right now.

"Bullet, you are going to make Colt Stevens a great quarter horse," I whisper. "I just hope he can see that."

When I leave for school, the two horses are on opposite ends of the yard. They aren't fighting. But they sure aren't acting like friends.

★ ★ ★

"Wait until you see what I got Colt for his birthday!" Larissa exclaims.

We're at lunch on Thursday. All anybody can talk about is Colt's birthday party. And Colt isn't even here to enjoy it.

"I still can't believe I'm going to miss the whole party," Ashley complains. "I wish Dad wouldn't make me go to that horse show in Breckenridge. What did you get Colt, Larissa?"

Larissa shakes her head. "I'm not telling. One of

you might spoil the surprise." She looks at me a second too long. "But I'll give you a clue—electronic!"

"Electronic?" Cassie repeats.

"And handheld," Larissa adds. "But that's all I'm saying."

They bat around other ideas for gifts. I keep my mouth shut. I don't want anybody to know what my gift is until Colt sees Bullet for himself.

Ethan beats me home after school. I find him sitting on our front step, watching the building going up across the street.

I sit beside him and stare into Colt's yard. *Wow! How did they build it so fast?* The entire frame is up, filled in, with a big door in front and high windows. Through the front windows you can see a loft upstairs and stalls downstairs.

Are you sure Colt's parents don't know he's getting a horse for his birthday? Ethan signs.

How could they?

115

Maybe they saw Bullet and figured it out. He shields his eyes from the sun for a better look. *It's definitely a barn.*

I shake my head. *No way. They started building before we got Bullet.*

I don't think I'll ever understand Colt's parents. Maybe they're just building that thing to make their place look better. Maybe they're running out of room in the garage for all Mr. Stevens's toys. He has a mini tractor, a riding mower, weed whackers, power washers. Maybe he's going to collect more antique cars or something. He used to try to get Colt to work on old fancy cars with him. But Colt was never into cars. He's like me. He would rather have a horse.

Friday night we're all at the ballpark an hour early. The Bear is already there. He and Ethan's coach are eating hot dogs, although the snack stand isn't even open yet.

When the other team arrives, the Bear leaves the field and comes to sit with us in the bleachers. He's showing teeth. I'm almost sure he's smiling.

We stand for the national anthem. Then the announcer introduces the players from both sides.

I know this is a Youth League game. These kids are just second graders. The only people in the stands are families of the kids. But it still feels like the World Series to me.

The scratchy speakers squeal. Then the announcer says, "And the starting home pitcher will be Ethan James."

We're on our feet, screaming so loud we drown out the groans of a few parents who must have seen my brother pitch in the last game.

"Do you think I should sit in the dugout or behind the plate to sign for Ethan?" I ask the Bear.

He leans down to answer. "Neither. He knows the catcher's signs. That's all he needs, just like every pitcher."

I've never thought about that. Baseball players have their own sign language. Maybe Ethan has an advantage there.

Mom, Dad, the Bear, and I are on our feet for Ethan's first pitch. It's a strike. We scream. Ethan has to at least feel the sound vibrations. Two more strikes, and the batter is out. Mom whistles so loud my ears ache.

After the third out, our Ethan is a hero. His teammates pat him on the back. They actually look like they're all friends . . . until Ethan bats.

I know that in some leagues pitchers don't have to bat. I wish my brother could switch to those leagues. He strikes out in three pitches.

"Can't help with that," the Bear mutters. "I didn't get to be the Bear by batting."

"That's okay," I tell him. "I have a friend, my best friend, who's a great batter. He'll help Ethan." I guess I'm kind of glad Ethan still needs Colt.

After three innings my brother has given up only two hits. No runs. Even I can see that his fastball is really fast. But his best pitches are the slow ones he surprises the batter with. Kids are striking before the ball reaches the plate. That's the changeup the Bear taught him.

When the coach starts to put Ethan in again for the bottom of the fourth inning, the Bear storms out of the bleachers and onto the field. Play stops until he has a word with the coach. Then there's a change of pitcher and Ethan has to go sit on the bench.

"Why did you do that?" I demand when the Bear gets back. "Ethan was doing great."

"If you want him to keep doing great, he has to take care of his arm. He's thrown enough pitches for one day." The Bear stares at me. I guess he can tell I don't like Ethan being on the bench again. "You want to know how Bullet has so much life left in him?"

I nod, hoping he's right about Bullet having a lot of life left.

"I rode him hard. But I always quit before I rode him out."

I think about that for a minute. "So you're saying Bullet can still, like, maybe do the barrels? Or run a figure eight?"

"You'll have to be careful until that weight comes off," the Bear warns. "But Bullet's still got his stuff. How 'bout I show you tomorrow morning?"

13

The Party

Saturday morning when I go out to the backyard, I sense something has changed. Then I notice what's different: Dream and Bullet are grazing just a couple of feet apart. You can't make two horses be friends any more than you can make two people be friends. But sooner or later, horses work it out. And it looks like that's what's happened with Dream and Bullet. Their tails switch together. And their ears flick from side to side–relaxed, not angry.

All horses need to know where they belong

in a herd. Even a herd of two. One has to be the leader, and the other agrees to follow. I can tell by the way Bullet keeps eyeing Dream that my horse is the leader. They have their pecking order set now. And both horses are happier. It's almost too bad Bullet has to live at Colt's.

I have time for a good ride before getting ready for Colt's party. Dream and I circle past the deserted farm at the end of our dirt road and come in the other side of town. I'm thinking I'll make a morning ride part of every day.

When I lead my horse into the backyard, Ethan meets me at the gate. He holds up his hand to stop me.

I start to protest. Then I see why.

The Bear is mounted on Bullet. They're standing square in the middle of the yard. Bullet's Western saddle is the old-school kind, leather and hand carved, with covers on the wooden stirrups and a super-wide saddle horn, where cowboys would loop ropes for lassoing cows.

I wouldn't have thought it was possible, but the Bear looks like a real cowboy.

Bullet stands still as a statue. His ears point straight ahead. His front hooves line up straight, and so do the back ones.

"Pivot left," the Bear calls.

Instantly Bullet swings both forelegs to the left. He barely shifts his hindquarters.

"Pivot right!" Before the Bear even has the words out, his horse responds. Then, with a tiny turn of the Bear's wrist, Bullet picks up the signal and pivots in a full circle.

The Bear has Bullet move backward. The horse keeps backing fast until the Bear says, "Whoa."

They face the back of the yard. Then they take off at a gallop, weaving around invisible barrels, before turning a perfect figure eight.

The Bear pulls up his horse inches from us. "Whoa, boy." In one smooth motion, he dismounts. "That's it until the old boy loses weight. You make sure your friend knows to go easy."

I'm as silent as Ethan. Speechless. Bullet is the perfect horse for Colt. It's what he has always dreamed of.

Colt's home! Ethan signs.

I'm brushing my hair, trying to get it to stay out of my face. But the humidity has my stray curls dancing every which way. I've decided on a red shirt that's one of my favorites. And blue jeans. I thought about shorts. But I'm hoping Colt might want to go for a ride with me after everybody leaves.

Ethan shifts from foot to foot. I don't think he's used to seeing me stand in front of a mirror this long. *I saw Colt's dad drive him in a minute ago.*

He almost missed his own party. Are you taking Bullet over there?

I give up on my hair. *No. I'll wait until everybody else goes home. Then I'll bring Colt over here. I need to do one last thing.*

Ethan follows me to Mom's ribbon drawer in the hall closet. I take a whole roll of green, Colt's favorite color, and a pair of scissors. Together Ethan and I tie Bullet into the lean-to so Colt won't see him and spoil the surprise. Then we fasten a big bow around his neck.

"Sorry, boy," I tell him, scratching right where he likes it. "You're a real cow horse. And I'll never make you wear a bow again. Promise."

Cassie and Rashawn pile out of Cassie's car as I walk up to Colt's house. I wave, and they wave back and wait for me.

Rashawn's carrying a big box wrapped in cute cowboy paper.

"We both went in on the present," Cassie says. "It's a rope thing. Like a cowboy's lariat. Colt can learn rope tricks with it."

"It comes with a book on doing rope tricks and everything. Do you think Colt will like it?" Rashawn asks.

"He'll *love* it!" It's all I can do not to spill my secret to them. I can see Cassie looking for my gift. But they don't ask.

Mrs. Stevens is standing on the front porch, welcoming everyone. She looks friendlier than I've ever seen her. "Come on in, girls! We've got lemonade on the table. And all kinds of snacks."

I nod to her as we walk by. But she's already greeting the kids behind us.

We walk in, and the whole place is lit up like Christmas. Little lights run from one end of the hall all through the house. Streamers form a paper tent over the huge dining table. And there must be a hundred balloons floating around everywhere.

"Wow!" Cassie says.

Rashawn and I just stare until the boys behind us shove us farther into the room. "I've never seen so much food!" Rashawn says. I agree.

Colt's dad walks in from the kitchen. At least a dozen backpacks dangle from his outstretched arms. And not just any backpacks. They're leather. Real leather. "Did you girls get your party favors yet?"

Cassie pulls one off the end of Mr. Stevens's arm. "These are party favors? For us?"

"Just a little something I picked up for Colt's friends this weekend." He hands one to Rashawn and one to me. Then he glances at his wife.

She glares back. I'm thinking she didn't know

about the packs and doesn't like the idea much. But I take one anyway.

"These must have cost more than our gift," Rashawn whispers.

We're still looking at the backpacks when Colt's mom rushes in with a basketful of real footballs and basketballs. "Help yourselves!" she shouts. "One for each of Colt's guests."

The guys grab for the footballs and basketballs. So do the girls. There are pink basketballs and striped footballs too. When they're almost gone, Cassie takes three of the balls that are left and puts one in each of our packs.

"Unbelievable, huh?" Cassie says. "Larissa kept saying this was going to be some party. Guess she was right."

I look around for Larissa and find her talking to Colt's mom. Mrs. Stevens looks like she wants to escape.

Before long the guys are all outside playing football with Mr. Stevens. Some of the girls are shooting baskets. Colt is out with the guys. I haven't even gotten a chance to wish him happy birthday yet.

I've gone back for a refill on the lemonade when I hear Mrs. Stevens shouting, "I told you to be here at one o'clock sharp!"

I glance into the kitchen. She's standing at the counter, her back to me. And she's screaming into her cell. "You'd better be here in ten minutes, or I'm not paying you a penny for the delivery. Do you hear me?"

I'm thinking the poor person on the other end of the phone could hear her without a phone. I move away from the door.

Two minutes later a sweet, smiling version of Mrs. Stevens calls outside, "Come in for gifts and cake, boys and girls!"

"We're in the middle of a game, Moira!" Mr. Stevens hollers back.

"Come in anyway!" she shouts. "Colt? Now."

Everybody sits around the big table. Mrs. Stevens lights the candles, and we all sing for Colt. Colt looks like he'd rather disappear under the table. Mrs. Stevens tells him to start opening the presents while she serves us cake and ice cream.

"Mine first!" Larissa shouts. She practically shoves her package into Colt's face.

He opens it and stares into the box. "Man, Larissa, this is too much."

"I know!" she agrees. "But isn't it cool?" She pulls it out of the box. It's some kind of handheld electronic game. Everybody oohs at the same time. "I have one just like it, but in pink," Larissa says.

I'm not that into games, but most of the kids seem to know what it is. And they wish they had one too.

Colt thanks her and moves on to the pile of gifts in front of him. All the presents are great. I admit that I'm starting to feel bad that I don't have anything for him here.

Suddenly Colt's dad turns from the window. "Colt! Your present is about to arrive!"

"What?" Mrs. Stevens frowns.

He doesn't answer her. He runs to Colt and almost drags him out of the chair. "Wait until you see what your old man got you!"

Colt and his dad rush outside. We all follow them.

"Wow!"

"No way!"

"Colt!"

I hear the shouts before I get outside. Then I see why. A black horse trailer pulls up in front of the house.

"Hold on a minute!" Mrs. Stevens cries. "That's *my* gift!"

But as she says it, a second horse trailer pulls onto our street. It parks behind the first one.

"He's getting *two* horses?" Larissa says.

Mr. and Mrs. Stevens glare at each other. Colt stands between them.

The driver of the first truck lets down the tailgate and leads out a beautiful sorrel American saddle horse mare. The horse is gorgeous. But she won't stand still. She dances in circles and pulls back on the lead rope so hard I'm afraid she's going to rear up and break it.

"It's a top-notch three-gaited American saddle horse," Colt's dad explains. "I had an associate in Kentucky find her for me. She has won all kinds of prizes already."

The horse in the second truck backs out of the

trailer. It's a fantastic bay mare at least seventeen hands high.

Colt's mother says, "Happy birthday, darling! I got you a *five*-gaited American saddle horse." She says this like she's proud of the extra two gaits.

Colt turns and faces us. His expression isn't excited. It isn't anything. "Thank you for coming, everybody. Thanks for all the presents, too. I hope you had a good time."

For a second nobody leaves. Then we all get the message at the same time. Kids start moving out. Some are texting or phoning their parents to come get them early. A couple of parents are already here. Some kids live close enough to walk home. It doesn't take long for the Stevenses' lawn to empty.

But I haven't budged. I keep looking at Colt, willing him to turn around and talk to me. I can't imagine him with two horses, much less three. An image of chubby Bullet pops into my head. He'd look even fatter next to these trim mares. Still, I can't picture Colt with either one of these horses.

Colt's parents are yelling at each other.

"He's keeping *my* horse!" Mrs. Stevens shouts. "That means *your* horse can go back where it came from!"

"That's not your decision! Colt can choose for himself!" Mr. Stevens shouts back.

Colt is watching them, barely looking at his gift horses.

I move next to him. "Colt, don't they know all you ever wanted was a quarter horse? How could they not know that? That's all you've talked about ever since we were friends."

He wheels on me. "What do you know about it? Some friend you are! You didn't even bother to get me a gift!"

Tears spring to my eyes. I've never seen Colt

this angry . . . and he's angry at *me*. I want to tell him he's wrong. I did get him a gift.

Only why make it worse? What made me think I could give *this* Colt—the Colt I don't even know anymore—a gift he'd really like?

14

Friends

I take off running across the road. I don't stop until I'm back to the house and in my bedroom. I throw myself onto my bed and cry and cry.

I don't know how long I've been crying when I hear a *thump, thump*. I stop my sobs. Then I hear it again. *Thump, thump.*

It's coming from my window.

I look up and see Dream's nose pressed against my window. I go over to her and lift the window. And just like that, she sticks her head all the way in.

I hug her and press my face next to hers. She did it! She came in when I needed her most.

There's a knock at the door.

"I'm busy!" I call.

There's another tap. Then the door opens. Ethan and Colt are standing there.

Way to go, Dream, Ethan signs. Then he leaves me alone with Colt.

Colt steps in. "I see you got her to stick her head in after all."

I nod.

"I'm sorry I said that about no present, Ellie. That was stupid. And mean. I was just messed up. I guess I've been messed up for a while."

"Why? What's wrong, Colt?" I ask, not letting go of Dream. "Why aren't we friends anymore?"

He looks up like I've smacked him. "We are! Aren't we?"

"I don't know," I admit. "You've sure been acting like we aren't. If we were friends, wouldn't you have told me what was wrong?"

Colt sits in the only chair in my room. "I couldn't." He's quiet for so long that I think he's done. Then, without looking at me, he says, "My parents are splitting up. They're getting a divorce."

"Colt . . ." I don't know what to say.

"That's why I had to go with Dad to St. Louis. He's got an apartment there already. He wanted to show me where I'll be visiting every other weekend. He's getting a house, and Sierra's going to live with him. She actually likes the idea. My sister always wanted to live in a city."

I want to ask him why he didn't tell me. But I think he just wants to talk. So I let him.

"It feels like I'm losing my dad *and* my sister." He pauses. "Sierra could change her mind still. And I guess I could change mine and go live with Dad."

I know it's selfish, but that makes me feel worse than anything.

"That's why Mom and Dad have been pulling out the super-parent act," he explains. "You saw how they were with those horses they got me. It's been like that with everything. I'm so tired of it. I told them both I don't even want their horses. You were right. I don't want a fancy English show horse. And neither one of them knows me well enough to know that."

"Colt, I can't believe you told them you don't want either horse. They must have cost thousands of dollars."

"Probably. But they're still not what I want. Those horses would never be like Dream. Can you imagine either one of them putting her head through my window?" We laugh a tiny bit. "I want a horse that will be a friend. Like Dream is to you."

"Do you mean it?"

"Yeah."

I kiss Dream on the head and turn to Colt. "Then maybe it's time to show you the present I got you."

"You don't have to do that, Ellie. I didn't mean–"

"You didn't really believe I wouldn't get a gift for my best friend, did you?" I ask.

He shrugs. "I wouldn't have blamed you if you didn't. I haven't been acting much like a friend."

"Follow me." I lead Colt through the house, right past Mom, Dad, and Ethan. They're supposed to be watching the Bear's first car commercial on TV. But I can tell they're all watching us and pretending not to.

At the back door I stop. "Colt, now you need to use your imagination before you see my present."

"I ought to be able to handle that. I've been hanging out with you long enough."

I walk toward the lean-to.

Colt follows me. "Where are we going?"

I don't answer. My heart is pounding. I walk into the lean-to and lead Bullet out. "Before you say anything, remember to use your imagination. This is Bullet. He has some extra weight on him— well, you can see that. But underneath that is a terrific quarter horse. He used to belong to the Bear, and—"

"The Bear?" Colt says. "As in the baseball legend the Bear?"

"Yeah. That's a long story. The Bear is Ethan's friend. Anyway, Bullet can pivot and do figure eights and everything. And the best part is . . . he'll be a friend, Colt. Like Dream is."

Colt is staring at Bullet. I can't tell what he's thinking.

"Okay," I say, "I know he's fat. And I guess he's a backyard horse. I mean, he's not a show horse.

But he was a working cow horse on a real ranch. And I'll bet you could get him in show condition. I mean, if you wanted to keep him." I picture the two perfect horses Colt just said no to. Could he ever say yes to this one?

"Ellie?" Colt says, still staring at Bullet.

"What?"

He walks up to Bullet. And the first thing he does is scratch the horse's jaw, right where he likes it. Bullet stretches his neck to beg for more. "I think he's about the finest horse I've ever seen."

I could be wrong, but I think Colt may be crying.

Together we saddle Bullet. Then Colt and I ride our horses. We keep it to a walk and don't leave my backyard. It's not the galloping-through-the-fields daydream I've imagined. But maybe it's even better. Colt and Bullet. Dream and me.

Four best friends.

*A friend is always loyal, and a brother
is born to help in time of need.*

Proverbs 17:17

Horse Talk!

Bay–A reddish-brown color for a horse. A bay horse usually has a black mane and tail.

Blaze–A facial marking on a horse (usually a wide, jagged white stripe).

Canter–A horse's slow gallop; a more controlled three-beat gait.

English–A style of horseback riding that is often considered more formal and classic than Western style. Riders generally sit on a flat saddle, post (rise from the saddle) on a trot, and hold the reins in both hands.

Farrier–Someone trained to care for a horse's hooves. Farriers trim hooves and put shoes on horses, but many also treat leg and tendon problems.

Foreleg–One of a horse's front legs.

Forelock–The piece of hair that falls onto a horse's forehead.

Gait–The way a horse moves, as in a walk, a trot, a canter, or a gallop.

Gallop–A horse's natural and fast running gait. It's speedier than a lope or a canter.

Gelding–A male horse that has had surgery so he can't mate and produce foals (baby horses). Geldings often make the calmest riding horses.

Habit–An outfit for horseback riding or showing, usually including some kind of tailored jacket and hat.

Halter–The basic headgear worn by a horse so the handler can lead the animal with a rope.

Hand–The unit for measuring a horse's height from the withers (area between the shoulders) to the ground. One hand equals four inches (about the width of an average cowboy's hand).

Hindquarters–The back end of a horse, where much of a horse's power comes from.

Hoof pick–A hooked tool, usually made of metal, for cleaning packed dirt, stones, and gunk from the underside of a horse's hoof.

Hunter–A horse that's bred to carry a rider over jumps. In a horse show, hunters are judged on jumping ability and style.

Lead rope–A length of rope with a metal snap that attaches to a horse's halter.

Lope–The Western term for *canter*. The lope is usually smooth and slower than the canter of a horse ridden English.

Mare–A female horse over the age of four, or any female horse that has given birth.

Nicker–A soft, friendly sound made by horses, usually to greet other horses or trusted humans.

Pinto–Any horse with patches or spots of white and another color, usually brown or black.

Quarter horse–An American horse breed named because it's the fastest horse for a quarter-mile distance. Quarter horses are strong and are often used for ranch work. They're good-natured and easygoing.

Saddle horse–A saddle horse could be any horse trained to ride with a saddle. More specifically, the American saddlebred horse is an elegant breed of horse used as three- and five-gaited riding horses.

Shetland pony–A small breed, no bigger than 10.2 hands, that comes from the Shetland Islands off Scotland. Shetland ponies are the ideal size for small children, but the breed is known to be stubborn and hard to handle.

Sorrel–A horse with a reddish-brown or reddish-gold coat.

Stallion–A male horse that hasn't had surgery to prevent him from mating and producing foals.

Swayback–A sagging back on a horse, or a horse with a deeply dipped back. Being swayback is often a sign of old age in a horse.

Three-gaited–Used to describe an American saddlebred horse that has been trained to perform at a walk, trot, and canter.

Throatlatch–The strap part of the bridle that helps keep the bridle on. It goes under a horse's throat, running from the right ear and loosely fastening below the left ear.

Trot–The two-beat gait where a horse's legs move in diagonal pairs. A trot is generally a choppy ride.

Western–A style of horseback riding used by cowboys in the American West. Western horseback riders usually use heavier saddles with saddle horns and hold both reins in one hand.

Whicker–A low sound made by a horse. A whicker is sometimes thought to be a cross between a whinny and a nicker.

Whorl–A twist of hair that grows in the opposite direction from the surrounding coat. This patch is usually on a horse's forehead.

Withers–The top of a horse's shoulders, between the back and the neck. The height of a horse is measured from the withers to the ground.

Sign Language Alphabet

A

B

C

D

E

F

G

H

I

J

K

L

M

N

O

P

Q

R

S

T

U

V

W

X

Y

Z

About the Author

Dandi Daley Mackall grew up riding horses, taking her first solo bareback ride when she was three. Her best friends were Sugar, a pinto; Misty, probably a Morgan; and Towaco, an Appaloosa. Dandi and her husband, Joe; daughters, Jen and Katy; and son, Dan (when forced), enjoy riding Cheyenne, their paint. Dandi has written books for all ages, including Little Blessings books, *Degrees of Guilt: Kyra's Story*, *Degrees of Betrayal: Sierra's Story*, *Love Rules*, *Maggie's Story*, the Starlight Animal Rescue series, and the bestselling Winnie the Horse Gentler series. Her books (about 450 titles) have sold more than 4 million copies. She writes and rides from rural Ohio.

Visit Dandi at www.dandibooks.com.

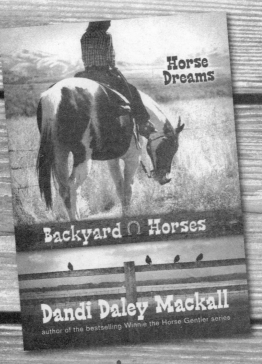